ALL ABOUT MAY
May's Too-Big Pizza

Written by A. T. Woehling
Illustrated by Felicia Whaley

Ready-to-Read

Simon Spotlight
New York   Amsterdam/Antwerp   London
Toronto   Sydney/Melbourne   New Delhi

To Harmonie—the world's biggest pizza lover.
May your days be saucy, your jokes be cheesy,
and your crust never betray you.
—F. W.

SIMON SPOTLIGHT
An imprint of Simon & Schuster Children's Publishing Division
1230 Avenue of the Americas, New York, New York 10020
For more than 100 years, Simon & Schuster has championed authors and the stories they create.
By respecting the copyright of an author's intellectual property, you enable Simon & Schuster and the author
to continue publishing exceptional books for years to come. We thank you for supporting
the author's copyright by purchasing an authorized edition of this book.
No amount of this book may be reproduced or stored in any format, nor may it be uploaded to any website,
database, language-learning model, or other repository, retrieval, or artificial intelligence system without
express permission. All rights reserved. Inquiries may be directed to Simon & Schuster, 1230 Avenue of the
Americas, New York, NY 10020 or permissions@simonandschuster.com.
This Simon Spotlight edition October 2025
Text © 2025 by A. T. Woehling
Illustrations © 2025 by Felicia Whaley
All rights reserved, including the right of reproduction in whole or in part in any form.
SIMON SPOTLIGHT, READY-TO-READ, and colophon are registered trademarks of Simon & Schuster, LLC.
For information about special discounts for bulk purchases, please contact Simon & Schuster Special Sales at
1-866-506-1949 or business@simonandschuster.com.
Simon & Schuster strongly believes in freedom of expression and stands against censorship in all its forms.
For more information, visit BooksBelong.com.
Manufactured in the United States of America 0925 LAK
10 9 8 7 6 5 4 3 2 1
CIP data for this book is available from the Library of Congress.
ISBN 9781665942881 (hc)
ISBN 9781665942874 (pbk)
ISBN 9781665942898 (ebook)

My family is a mess.
A BIG mess!

When we make pancakes,
they get bigger
and bigger
and BIGGER!

When we go shopping, the list gets longer and longer and LONGER!

When we play music, it gets louder and louder and LOUDER!

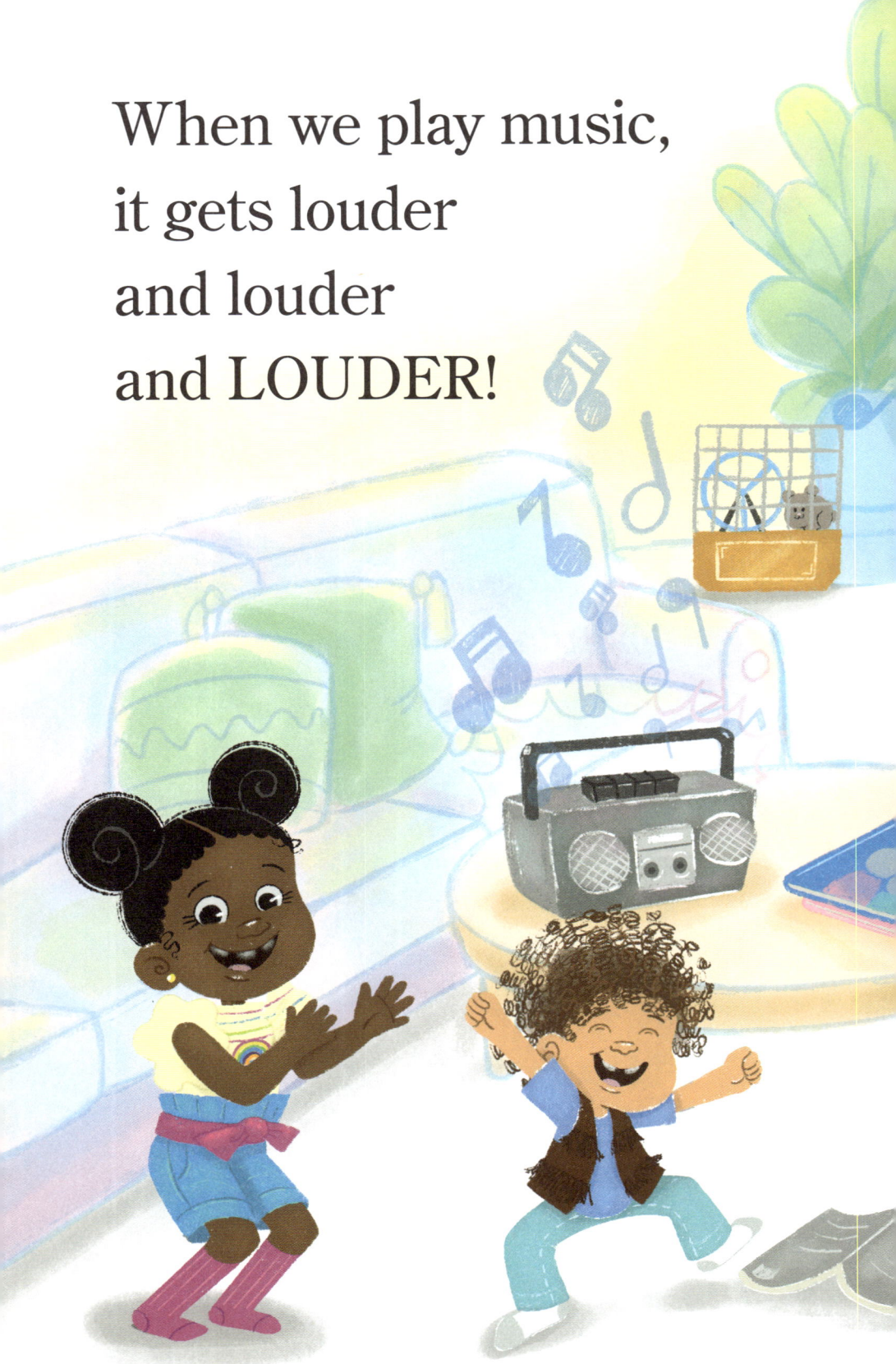

We are always TOO big!

But today my friend Stella is here! She is going to help us make pizza.

We need a pizza,
a REALLY big pizza.
But not TOO big!

We need flour,
a lot of flour.
But not too much!

We need dough,
a lot of dough.
But not too stretchy!

This is getting
TOO big,
too big for me!

We need sauce,
a lot of sauce.
But not too saucy!

We need cheese,
a lot of cheese.
But not too cheesy!

This is getting TOO big,
too big for me!

We need pepper, a lot of pepper. But not too spicy!

We need garlic,
a lot of garlic.
But not too stinky!

This is getting
TOO big,
too big for me!

We need vegetables,
a lot of vegetables.
But not too many!

We need oil,
a lot of oil.
But not too slippery!

This is TOO big!
Way too big for me!

"Your family is big and messy, for sure. But I have NEVER had this much fun before!

Let us just try a bite, a slice or two. Then we can go do something small, just me and you!"

This pizza is big, really big.
But it's never too big for me!